Mr. Arc is Missing!

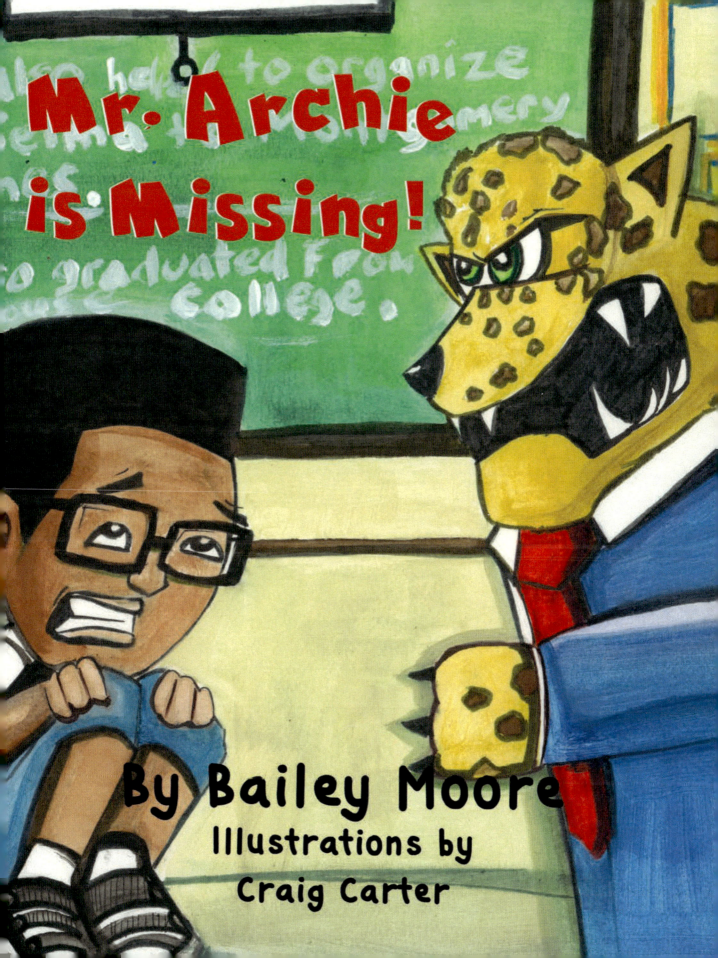

Copyright © 2018 by B-Moore-U Publishing

Bailey C. Moore
P.O. Box 321191 Houston, TX 77221-1191

www.baileycmoore.com
info@baileycmoore.com

Mr. Archie is Missing

ISBN: 978-0-692-98444-4

Printed in the United States of America. All rights reserved. No part of this publication may be reproduced, stored in a retrieval system, or transmitted in any form or by any means—electronically, mechanically, photocopying, recording, or any other— except for brief quotations in printed reviews, without the prior permission of the publisher.

Illustrations by Craig Carter
Book Production: Marvin D. Cloud

This book belongs to:

_____

From:

_____

I dedicate this book to the world's best mom—my mother, Qiana Moore.

Acknowledgments

I thank my mother, Qiana Moore, who taught me about respect. I also thank my uncles, Patrick Wiltz, Jerald Robins, and Marc Boone. They showed me how to respect myself, as well as, others and to focus on being a better person. I am grateful to Coach D, Coach Ben, Coach Trae, and Coach Jerald for showing me how to respect my teammates on and off the football field. In addition, there is a special place in my heart for Coach Kevin and Coach Ken. Last but not least, I thank my aunts: Lynn, Stacy, Tracy, Tamara, and Dominick for supporting me, along with, MehaffyWeber P.C.

"Never trade respect for attention."

Meet Jerry ...

Jerry Jones always enjoyed being the center of attention at Moore Academy. He was an only child and at his school, he enjoyed playing jokes on his friends and teachers. He especially enjoyed playing practical jokes in the history class taught by Mr. Archie.

One time, Jerry put toothpaste in a bag of Oreos that belonged to his friend, Brandon. Another time, Jerry put whoopie cushions in everyone's chair. Jerry laughed so hard that day.

He even put itching powder in Brandon's new shirt and scared another friend, Jeremiah, in the dark hallway when bad weather made the lights go out.

Mr. Archie was the students' favorite teacher at Moore Academy. He was the type of teacher who wasn't too strict, but he was respected all around by the students and the faculty. Although Jerry loved history, he had a reputation to uphold as being the school's funniest kid in third grade.

Every Friday was Mr. Archie's history class and Jerry would go into the room ready to be the class clown. He could pull the funniest pranks and Mr. Archie would never send him to the office. Mr. Archie believed in the students expressing themselves.

Today was about Black History. Mr. Archie was halfway into the history lesson about Dr. Martin Luther King Jr., when Jerry gave out a big burp.

"BURRPP!"

The whole class burst into laughter.

"Who was that?" asked Mr. Archie.

Jerry didn't say a word, but he looked at Mr. Archie with a slick grin. Normally, he was an easy-going teacher and would let it go. This time, Jerry could see in Mr. Archie's eyes, he had enough of him disrupting the class.

He said, "One day you will regret your actions, Jerry."

Jerry rolled his eyes and looked around the class for approval and confirmation that he was indeed the funniest kid in third grade.

That night, Jerry put on his pajamas. He could not sleep. He couldn't get the look that Mr. Archie had in his eyes, out of his head. As he drifted to sleep, he thought about how badly he felt.

When it was time for history class again, Jerry walked down the hall. He didn't see Mr. Archie at the door where he normally greeted the students. He didn't hear any sounds coming from the classroom where the children usually would be playing and talking. But like clockwork, Jerry entered into Mr. Archie's class ready for the laughter of approval from his fellow classmates.

But this time something felt differently. Instead of Mr. Archie, he saw a creature.

"Hi, I'm Mr. Stanley, your teacher," the creature said. Jerry was surprised.

Actually, the whole class was surprised! A big jaguar was their teacher. The jaguar smiled and showed his sharp teeth.

How could this be? Where was Mr. Archie?

Class went by slowly. Jerry thought to himself, *I'm not scared of a jaguar.* He tried to think of the funniest thing he could do to get his friends to laugh.

He decided to mock everything the new teacher did behind his back. But nothing worked. No one laughed.

However, the jaguar did react. He saw Jerry and growled at the top of his lungs, "Jerry go to the office right now!" His eyes appeared evil.

Jerry left the class quickly and ran to the principal's office.

When he arrived, the principal said, "Jerry, I'm surprised you are in here."

Jerry was surprised as well. He had never gotten in trouble in spite of all of his foolish pranks. He tried to tell the principal, Mrs. Harvey, that the new teacher was a jaguar, but she would not listen.

Instead, she called his parents and they put him on punishment.

That whole week went by slowly. Jerry thought, *If Mr. Archie was here, this would have never happened.* And what about his friends?

Why didn't they notice Mr. Stanley was a jaguar? When next Friday came, Jerry hoped Mr. Stanley was not in the classroom. But as he entered the door, he saw the furry Mr. Stanley writing again on the chalkboard.

He looked at Jerry with those same eyes and told him to sit in the corner. Jerry was mad, and he had an attitude. He sat in the back of the class.

He was bored and thought about how Mr. Archie would have been telling cool stories about history and showing the class all of the special items he had collected. Jerry really missed Mr. Archie and wished he had never disrupted his class. He wished he could show Mr. Archie how important he was to him.

When school was over, Jerry was happy. He said to himself, *I hope I never see that Mr. Stanley again.* When Friday rolled around, Jerry was nervous about history class.

Again Mr. Stanley was there. Every Friday he had the same mean stare. And he always seemed to pick on Jerry and send him to the office.

It had been weeks since Mr. Archie was in history class. Jerry was tired of being picked on. Still, every Friday he got into trouble.

One day as he was walking out of the school, he noticed a sign that said, "One day you will regret your actions." And it hit Jerry, Mr. Archie was right. He regretted how he always disrupted his class.

He wanted another chance to prove to Mr. Archie that he could change. As he looked at the sign again, the bell rang… or so he thought. When he looked at himself he was still in his pajamas.

It was all a dream. Jerry rushed to get ready for school. He brushed his teeth, washed his face, put on his clothes, said goodbye to his parents, and ran to school.

As he walked to Mr. Archie's class he saw his favorite teacher standing at the door. Jerry ran to Mr. Archie and gave him a big hug and apologized. Jerry told Mr. Archie about his dream.

Jerry and Mr. Archie talked and laughed until it was time for class to begin. Jerry learned a valuable lesson. From that day on he treated others with respect.

The End ...
or is it?

About The Author

Bailey C. Moore is a nine-year old from Houston, Texas. Like most young boys, Bailey enjoys spending time with his friends, along with playing football, video games, and, of course, reading and writing. At a young age Bailey's mother introduced him to books and his grandfather introduced him to writing, which began his love for both.

Bailey decided he wanted to write a children's book after watching his mother put up a vision board of her goals for the 2017 year. He decided he wanted to work towards his goals, as well. At the top on his list was to become an author.

Bailey maintains a straight A Grade Point Average while playing football with the South Side Cowboys and running track with The Houston Pace Setters. Bailey gives thanks to the many influential people in his life who have made his dream come true.

Respect

When asked to define the word "Respect," Bailey said, "I first think of respect as being 'Treating others the way you want to be treated.'" He continued, "I also think of respect as loyalty. Respect is helping each other and being nice to each other. *Mr. Archie is Missing* is about respect. I wrote this book to show how when you respect others you will be treated well and will get the *right* attention."

Our Mission

B-MOORE-U Publishing's vision is to:

- Assist authors with their writing goals.
- Be a publisher that values hard work, diversity, and holds high standards of quality for our products.
- Create content that educates, informs, and inspires.

Help Bailey Spread The Message of Respect

Buy this book for the children in your life!

$15.⁹⁹

Plus $4 S&H
& $1.65 tax

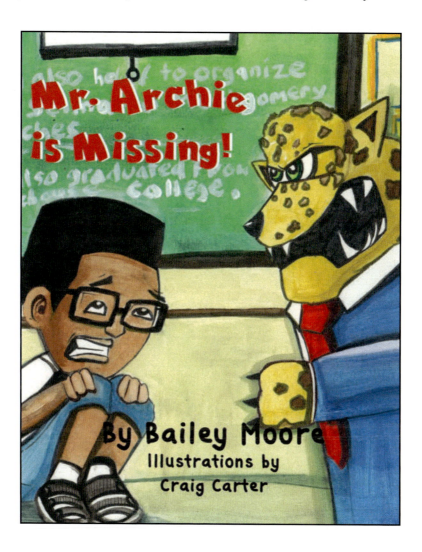

Visit: www.baileycmoore.com

or send check or money order to:

B-Moore-U Publishing
P.O. Box 321191 Houston, TX 77221-1191

Made in the USA
Coppell, TX
16 May 2022